FIELD TRIP MYSTERIES

The Cave That Shouldn't Collapse

by
Steve Brezenoff
illustrated by
Marcos Calo

STONE ARCH BOOKS
a capstone imprint

f Samantha Archer,

Field Trip Mysteries are published by Stone Arch Books
A Capstone Imprint
1710 Roe Crest Drive
North Mankato, Minnesota 56003
www.capstonepub.com

Library of Congress Cataloging-in-Publication Data
Brezenoff, Steven.
The cave that shouldn't collapse / by Steve Brezenoff ; illustrated by Marcos Calo.
p. cm. -- (Field trip mysteries)
ISBN-13: 978-1-4342-3227-4 (library binding)
ISBN-10: 1-4342-3227-1 (library binding)
ISBN-13: 978-1-4342-3430-8 (pbk.)
ISBN-10: 1-4342-3430-4 (pbk.)
1. Caves--Juvenile fiction. 2. Gems--Juvenile fiction. 3. School field trips--Juvenile fiction. 4. Detective and mystery stories. [1. Mystery and detective stories. 2. Caves--Fiction. 3. School field trips--Fiction. 4. Gems--Fiction.] I. Calo, Marcos, ill. II. Title. III. Title: Cave that should not have collapsed. IV. Series: Brezenoff, Steven. Field trip mysteries.
PZ7.B7576Cav 2011
813.6--dc22
2011002173

Art Director/Graphic Designer:
Kay Fraser

Summary: On a science class trip to a local cave, Edward "Egg" Garrison and his friends are confronted by the mystery of a faked cave-in.

Printed in the United States of America
in Stevens Point, Wisconsin.
072012
006847R

TABLE OF CONTENTS

Chapter One
THE ARTICLES? 7

Chapter Two
NO GOLD 13

Chapter Three
DANGEROUS 18

Chapter Four
A CRIME TO FIND 25

Chapter Five
TOO LAZY 31

Chapter Six
RULE-BREAKER 36

Chapter Seven
CATS AND KITTENS 47

Chapter Eight
TROUBLEMAKERS 50

Chapter Nine
HAMMY 57

Chapter Ten
BIG TONY 62

Chapter Eleven
WORTHLESS? 69

STUDENTS
Edward G. Garrison
A.K.A: Egg
D.O.B: May 14th
POSITION: 6th Grade
This can't be correct.
Please confirm.
INTERESTS:
Photography, field trips
KNOWN ASSOCIATES:
Archer, Samantha; Duran, Catalina;
and Shoo, James.
NOTES:
Ms. Stanwyck encourages Edward's
passion for photography, but some
teachers complain of the frequent
use of the flash.
Is photography allowed in school? I will
look into this.

CAVES OF THE STATE

THE ARTICLES?

Before I get started, let me introduce myself. I'm Edward G. Garrison, better known as Egg. And my friends Cat, Gum, and Sam and I love field trips. But the thing is, we usually end up solving a mystery or two while we're on them.

This Tuesday morning, the bus pulled up to Buckaroo Cavern. "Okay, everyone," Mr. Neff said. "Off the bus, please."

My friends and I always sat in the back of the bus, so we were the last ones to get off. As we passed the driver, Cat stopped to talk to him. She's always very friendly.

"Ooh, I love cats," she said in her sweetest voice. The driver was reading an issue of *Cats and Kittens*. Cat — short for Catalina — loves almost all animals, but cats are probably her favorite.

The driver grunted in response, but didn't look up from his magazine. He was a very big man, hairy as a gorilla. We've seen most bus drivers a bunch of times, but we didn't recognize this guy.

"Do you have cats at home?" Cat asked. "I have three."

She counted off on her fingers, saying, “Peanut, the orange one. Caramel, the tan one. And of course Midnight, the black one. She has a white spot like the moon on her belly.” She smiled up at the driver, waiting for him to reply.

Finally the driver lowered his magazine. His big, hairy face was red at the cheeks. “Who cares about cats?” he snapped.

Cat and I flinched. Gum stepped back. Even Sam jumped a little, and she's not easily startled.

"Um," Cat said. "You were just reading *Cats and Kittens* magazine."

The bus driver's jaw dropped. "Oh, right," he stammered, trying to smile. "Great magazine. Yep. I really like the — uh — articles."

He got up from his seat and ushered us down the steps. "Time to get off the bus," he said. "Your class will start without you!"

The four of us stumbled down the bus steps. An instant later, the folding bus doors closed with a *hiss* and a *thwack*.

"Wow," Sam said. "That guy's cruising for a bruising."

"He sure isn't very pleasant," Cat said.

"I bet he
hates children,"
Gum said.

Cat nodded. "Mr. Neff said he's a temporary driver," she said. "He just started last week."

"Why would anyone like that want to drive a school bus?" I asked. I took a step back from the bus and snapped a photo of the bus driver through the closed door. He had gone back to reading his magazine.

"It's hard to believe he likes kittens," Cat said quietly.

Sam elbowed me. "He probably eats them," she said.

Cat shivered. "Let's catch up with Mr. Neff and the rest of the class," she said.

We walked across the parking lot toward a big, old-looking house.

On the way to the house, we passed the picnic area. We also saw some bright yellow digging equipment, like smaller versions of the big machines they use at construction sites.

We reached the house, and Mr. Neff led us inside. The front room was decorated like an Old West theme restaurant or something.

"The cavern owner is a man named Mesquite Buckaroo," Mr. Neff said. "Or is it Buckaroo Mesquite?"

Mr. Neff always got people's names wrong. He has called me Ham or Toast as often as he's called me Egg.

"Anyway," Mr. Neff went on, "he discovered the caves a long time ago and claimed them to look for gold. He never found any."

Mr. Neff walked over to the wall. Hanging there was a stuffed bat.

"Wow," Gum whispered to me. "I've seen stuffed deer before, even a buffalo, but I've never seen a stuffed bat."

"The cave was full of bats," Mr. Neff said. "Mr. Buckaroo got rid of all of them." He patted the stuffed bat like it was a puppy. "He stuffed this one as a reminder of who once ran that cave."

Mr. Neff sighed, like he really cared about those bats. "Alas, today there are no bats left in the cave," he said. "Instead, all the bats in this area now live in the bat sanctuary under Big Rock Hill. If the sanctuary loses its funding, it might not last long."

Anton Gutman, our class troublemaker, laughed in the back of the room. "If there's no gold," he said with a sneer, "then why did he keep the caves?" His goons laughed.

Mr. Neff cleared his throat. His face quickly went from sad to annoyed as he looked at Anton.

"Instead of gold, Mr. Buckaroo made his fortune by charging people to enter the caverns," Mr. Neff said. "He still does. Of course, he's quite old now, so he doesn't lead the tours himself anymore."

Just then, a teenage boy came out of the back room. "Nope," he said, frowning, "that's my job now. I'm Mr. Buckaroo's great-grandson, Andy, and I hate the stupid cave."

"Hello, Handy," Mr. Neff said.

"My name is Andy," the guide said again. "Not Handy!" He rolled his eyes. Then he headed for an exit on the other side of the main room. "Let's start the tour."

Outside, a path led away from the building. We followed Andy through some woods for a few steps. Then we came to the mouth of the cave.

"Cool," Sam said. Cat and Gum nodded, and I snapped a bunch of pictures.

The cave mouth was not what I thought it would be. I pictured a huge, gaping hole in the rock. But it was kind of small. It was only big enough for maybe two or three people to go in next to each other.

And inside wasn't dark — at least not where we could see from the outside. It seemed to glow red.

"The natural rocks in the cave are quite dull," Mr. Neff said. "The lights you see are simply colored light bulbs Mr. Buckaroo has hung near the entrance. Once we get deeper, it will be much darker, and much colder."

Andy went through the mouth of the cave. Mr. Neff stepped to the side to let the students in first.

Just past the mouth, Andy stopped. He pointed to the right. "We normally start the tour that way," he said. We all looked down the right path. Yellow tape blocked it off, like a crime scene. "However," Andy went on in a dry, bored voice, "that section is in danger of collapsing."

"Collapsing?"
Cat said, startled.

Andy nodded. "Great-grandpa closed that section last Thursday," he said. He pointed toward the yellow tape. "See all that gravel and debris? He says it shows the ceiling in there is crumbling. Very dangerous."

I stayed where I was and snapped a photo. Gum and Sam went over to the tape.

"Don't get too close," Andy said, but he didn't sound like he really cared that much. He didn't try to stop them from going over there.

"Can they get hurt?" Cat asked.

Andy shrugged. "I doubt it," he said. "Personally, I'm glad that section is closed. It's really steep. There are lots of steps. Ugh."

"Hey, Pam and Candy," Mr. Neff called out.

"Sam and Gum," I corrected him.

"Right," Mr. Neff said with a smile. "Just ask them to get back over here."

Andy started leading the class down to the left, away from the tape, just as Sam and Gum rejoined us.

"Anything interesting over there?" Cat asked as we followed the others.

Sam nodded. "Gum," she said, "show them what you found."

Gum held out a rock. It wasn't especially interesting to me, but I knew Gum must have picked it up for a good reason. He loves geology almost as much as Mr. Neff does.

"This rock," he said, "shouldn't be in this cave."

"Huh?" Cat said. "Where should it be? There are lots of rocks here. What's so special about this one?"

"It's not special, exactly," Gum said quietly. "The thing is, it's a volcanic rock. There are no volcanic rocks in this part of the country."

"Then how did it get here?" I asked. I snapped a photo of the big, gray rock. It had little holes all over it.

Gum shook his head. "I don't know," he said, "but it was with all that debris by the yellow tape."

"So someone had to put it here," Cat said.

Sam tapped her own nose. "Exactly," she said. "Maybe that section isn't crumbling at all. Someone just wants Mr. Buckaroo to think it is."

A CRIME TO FIND

Andy was leading the class down a steady slope, deeper into the caves. It had gotten kind of cold.

I made sure to take lots of photos with my digital camera. Whenever I did, my flash would light up the cave very briefly.

Mr. Neff was right, though. The inside of the cave was dark and dull. There was no color in it at all. In fact, so far, I was pretty bored with this whole field trip. It wasn't exciting at all.

"Why would anyone want Mr. Buckaroo to close a section of the cave?" Cat asked.

Sam pulled out her notebook and scribbled something down. "That's the question, Cat," she said. "Once we have the answer, we'll have our crook."

"Crook?" Gum repeated. "Is this even a crime?"

Sam smiled and patted Gum's shoulder. "This is just the surface, old friend," she said. "Behind this, there's got to be a real crime to solve. We just have to find it."

"If you say so," Gum said. "We can start by questioning Anton."

Cat, Sam, and I laughed. Gum glared at us.

"Oh, come on," Sam said. "You always want to question Anton. He's not a suspect!"

"Why not?"

Gum said. "He's definitely a troublemaker This is trouble. Maybe he made it."

Cat chewed her cheek. "We shouldn't rule him out," she said. "It is his style to cause trouble for its own sake."

"Okay," Sam said, "but right now, I have a stronger suspect. Someone with a motive."

"Who?" I asked.

"Our guide," Sam said. "Andy Buckaroo."

TOO LAZY

"No way. Andy would never do it," Gum said. He crossed his arms and shook his head. "Just doesn't make sense. It's his family's business. Why would he want to hurt something that means so much to his grandpa?"

"So what?" Sam said. "They're still giving tours. They're still charging admission. No big loss for the family."

I nodded. "That's true," I said. "But what's his motive?"

"Weren't you listening?" Sam said. "He's happy not to have to climb all those steps, and hates the cave."

"Yeah!" Cat said. Her face brightened. "He said so himself!"

Sam nodded and put an arm around Cat's shoulders. "Exactly," Sam said. "This could be our easiest case yet."

Gum shrugged. "Not much of a crime, though," he said. "He'll probably just get grounded."

Something occurred to me.

"But there's one thing wrong," I said. "Andy is lazy, right?"

"Right," Sam said. "That's why he doesn't want to lead the tour that way. He said it's too many stairs, or something."

"But isn't he too lazy to haul all that debris into the caves?" I said.

Gum and Cat stared at me. Sam scratched her chin.

"Remember," I said. "Gum explained that the debris didn't come from here. Someone brought it from somewhere else. That would take a lot of work."

Gum nodded and narrowed his eyes. "Rocks are heavy," he said.

Sam glanced at him. "Good point," she said. "Would there be an easy way for someone to move all those rocks?"

We thought for a minute. Suddenly Cat clapped and hopped up and down. "I know!" she said. "That digging equipment in the parking lot, near the picnic tables."

"Good thinking," Sam said. "We're about to break for lunch. We can check out the diggers before we start eating."

RULE-BREAKER

"There are the diggers," Cat said. She hurried ahead of us.

I guess she was excited that she'd thought of checking out the diggers. It was a pretty great idea. But her face went from very happy to very disappointed once she reached the equipment.

"Aw, man," Cat said.

Gum, Sam, and I caught up to her. "What's the problem?" I asked.

Cat put her hands out toward the diggers. "Well, look at them," she said. "They're brand new. I bet they've never been used."

"Hmm," Sam said. She kneeled next to a digger and ran her finger along its edge. "Not a scratch on them."

"Those rocks would have scratched this paint," Gum said. "Definitely."

I lifted my camera to take a few pictures, but just then, I felt someone grabbing my shoulder.

If the camera hadn't been on a strap around my neck, I probably would have dropped it.

"What are you kids doing?" Andy asked.

We spun around. "Nothing," Cat said quickly. "We were just, um, heading to lunch with our class."

MAC-1

I glanced at the tables. Everyone else from our class was already seated. It looked like they were all just starting to eat their bag lunches.

"Well, move it along, then," Andy said. "Get away from this equipment. It's dangerous."

"It doesn't look dangerous," Gum said.

"Yeah," Sam said. She put a hand on the shovel of a digger. "It looks like no one has ever turned them on."

Andy grabbed her by the wrist and pulled her away, toward the picnic tables. Gum, Cat, and I chased alongside them.

"That," Andy said, "is because they have never been used. The diggers are there in case there's a collapse in the cave. If some stupid kids get trapped, we'd have to dig them out."

I swallowed hard. "I guess you would," I said.

"Now eat," Andy said. Then he walked off.

"Boy, he's as nasty as our new bus driver," Cat said. She made a mean face at Andy as he walked away, when his back was to us.

Sam nodded. "He's still my number-one suspect," she said. "Lazy or not, he's on my list."

"There you four are," Mr. Neff said. "Sit down and take out your lunches."

I looked at the tables. They were totally full. "There's nowhere to sit," I said.

The teacher stood up and looked around. Across the parking lot was another table. "Well, we can't have you four sitting all the way over there," Mr. Neff said. He looked at the rest of the class.

"Who are the strongest students?" Mr. Neff asked. Anton's two goons stood up, smirking, and flexed their muscles.

"Great," Mr. Neff said. "Go and get that table. Carry it over here so our classmates can sit with us."

Mr. Neff sat back down and started eating. Anton's goons groaned, but they walked across the parking lot and heaved the table off the grass. Then they carried it back and dropped it near us. It landed with a thud.

"Dorks," one of them said quietly. The two of them went back to their table and sat next to Anton. He laughed at them.

My friends and I sat down at our table. Cat leaned forward and whispered, "Did you guys see that?" she said.

"We were standing right here," Gum said. "Of course we saw it."

"Anton's best friends," Cat went on, "are very strong."

"This is not news," Sam said. "What's your point?"

I smiled at Cat, then turned to Sam. "Don't you see?" I said. "They're strong enough to carry a big pile of rocks into the caverns."

Sam's confused look slowly became a smile.

"Finally," Gum said. "You're taking Anton seriously as a suspect, huh?"

Sam nodded. "We all know they usually work for Anton. We have to investigate those two goons," she said. "But how?"

"There's lots of personal property on the bus still," Cat pointed out. "One of us can slip on and check it out."

"It's too risky," Sam said. "Especially since Mr. Neff is a suspect too."

I nearly fell off the bench. "Mr. Neff?" I repeated. "Why?"

"Didn't you hear all that talk about the bat sanctuary?" Sam said. "He'd probably love to see the whole cave closed for good so the bats could come back."

Cat nodded. "Good point," she said. "Mr. Neff likes animals as much as I do. I wish the bats could live safely here too." She paused, then added, "But I'm not a suspect. I swear!"

“See?” Sam said. “I’d say he’s our strongest suspect.” She reached into her bag and pulled out her old black lunchbox.

“Definitely,” Gum said. “Which is why sneaking onto the bus is way too risky.” He opened up his brown paper lunch bag and took out his bologna sandwich.

I found my container of pasta salad in my bag and opened it up.

“Well, I’m not sneaking onto the bus,” I said. “Whoever does will definitely get in trouble.”

“I’ll go,” Cat said.

We all turned and stared at her. Gum stopped chewing in mid-chew.

“You?!” Sam said. “Cat, you never break rules like that.”

Cat shrugged. "It has to be me," she said. "I'm the only one who could do this without making Mr. Neff suspicious. Don't worry. I have a plan."

Cat hid her lunch bag under her shirt. Then she got up from the table and walked over to Mr. Neff. "I forgot my lunch on the bus," she said.

He glanced at her for a moment. "Then go get it, Bunny," he said.

"Um, it's Cat," she said.

"I'm sorry," Mr. Neff said, smiling. "Go ahead, Pat."

Cat laughed and headed toward the bus. On the way, she flashed a thumbs-up.

CATS AND KITTENS

Lunch was tense for a few long minutes. It seemed like Cat would never get back.

None of us spoke. We just ate our lunches and kept our eyes on the bus, waiting for Cat to come through the folding doors again.

Finally, after what seemed like hours, Cat stepped off the bus. She held up her lunch bag so everyone could see it, and called out, "Got it!"

Anton and his goons clapped slowly. "Way to go," Anton shouted. His friends laughed.

Cat just smiled at them and sat down with us. We leaned in.

"So?" Sam said. "What did you find?"

"Anything to incriminate Anton?" Gum asked. "Maybe an extra bag of rocks?"

"Or something in Mr. Neff's stuff?" I said. "Maybe he has been in touch with a bat rescue group!"

Cat shook her head and smiled. She unzipped her lunch bag and pulled out a magazine, then dropped it in front of us.

"*Cats and Kittens*?" Sam said. "What is this for? Some lunchtime reading?"

Cat giggled and unwrapped her cheese and tomato sandwich. "Open it," she said.

Sam gave her a twisted glare. I picked up the magazine.

As soon as I opened it, though, another magazine slid out and landed on the table.

"What's that?" Gum asked.

I picked it up and looked at the cover, then held it up for the others to see: *Gems and Jewels Price Guide Monthly*.

TROUBLEMAKERS

"Well, this is interesting," Sam said. "Our new bus driver was hiding his interest in gems. But why?"

"We should question him, right?" Cat asked. She looked proud that she'd found an important clue.

"This must be pretty strong evidence," I said, nodding at Cat. She smiled back at me.

Gum grabbed the gem and jewel magazine and flipped through the pages. He shrugged.

"Not really," he said. "Like Mr. Neff said, and from what I've seen so far, there's nothing in this cave worth harvesting and selling. It's made of worthless rocks. There aren't any gems there."

Most of the class had finished their lunches by then. A group of kids got up from one of the other tables.

"Hey, there go Anton and his goons," Gum said. He stood up. "Come on. We should follow them."

Cat had her sandwich in her mouth. She'd only taken a few bites. She stared up at Gum. "Um," she said. "I'm not done eating. Can we wait a minute?"

Sam shook her head. "Eat while we walk," she said.

"No time to waste," Gum said.

The four of us got up and followed Anton and his friends, staying way back and out of sight. Most of the class headed for the main building, where the gift shop was.

"They're not following the rest of the class," Gum said. "They're going back into the cave."

Sam flashed that smile she saves for when we're about to bust a crook. Gum smiled even bigger. "We're finally going to catch Anton in the act," Gum said. He rubbed his hands together like my dad does when my mom makes pot roast.

The three troublemakers entered the cave. It was no surprise when they headed toward the yellow tape and the closed-off section of the cave.

"There they go," Cat said.

She looked genuinely scared, like she was worried about them. "I hope they're careful," she said nervously. "It could be really dangerous in there."

"Are you serious?" I said. "The cave isn't really collapsing, remember?"

Cat shrugged. "They should still be careful," she said.

The four of us stepped into the cave as quietly as we could. Anton and his goons were just past the tape on our right. With their backs to us, they were trying to carve their names into the wall of the cave.

Sam put a finger to her lips so we'd know to keep quiet. We tiptoed toward the tape.

When we were right behind them, Sam coughed loudly and said, "What are you goons up to?"

Anton and his friends were so startled, they dropped the pocket knives they'd been using. When they were still standing there shocked, with their mouths hanging open, I snapped a picture of them.

"And that's all the evidence we need," Gum said. "You three are so busted."

Anton looked worried for a minute, but then he chuckled. "Like we're afraid of you nerds," he said. "If you try anything, my friends here will —"

"What friends?" Sam said.

I looked around. Sam was right. Anton's two goons had run off.

"There they go," Cat said, looking at the mouth of the cave.

"Sorry, Anton," one of them yelled as he fled from the cave.

"They have proof. I don't want them to get me in trouble," the other one called.

So Anton was alone. Sam took him by the arm. "Let's go," she said. "We'll hand you over to Mr. Neff."

HAMMY

The rest of our class was in the main building. We were out of breath from all the excitement when we found everybody.

"Where have you been?" Mr. Neff asked. "Stanley was about to finish the tour for us."

"Andy!" the tour guide said. "My name is Andy, not Stanley."

Mr. Neff smiled and patted him on the shoulder. "Of course it is, Hammy," he said. "Of course it is."

"Sorry, Mr. Neff," Sam said. "We just saw Anton and his friends go into the cave, so we thought that's where the whole class was."

Mr. Neff looked at Anton. "Just what were you up to in there?" Mr. Neff asked. "I told you we were heading to the gift shop next."

"Oh, um," Anton said. "I followed these dorks and they were . . ."

I switched on my camera and showed Anton the pictures I had of him vandalizing the cave.

"Doing nothing, Mr. Neff," Anton said. "Nothing at all. They explained to me that we should go to the main building, so here we are!" He flashed his best good-boy smile.

Mr. Neff looked doubtful, but he let it go. When he'd turned away and Anton had found his goons in the back, Sam poked me.

"I want to see that photo of Anton and his goons," she said. I flipped it on again and showed her. "Aha!"

"Aha what?" I said. I squinted at the photo. It just showed Anton vandalizing the cave.

She shook her head. "Give me the camera, quick," she said.

I pulled it off my neck and handed it to Sam. She hid it behind her back. "Hey, Mr. Neff!" Sam shouted.

The teacher turned to us again. "What is it now, Tim?" he said.

"Sam," Sam said, smiling. "And Egg lost his camera."

"No, I didn't," I started to say.

Gum elbowed me. "Yeah, we better get that camera," he said. "You know how Egg is about it. It's like his favorite thing."

"Yeah!" Cat said. "He needs it."

"I think he left it in the cave just now," Sam said. "While we were in there looking for Anton."

Andy sighed and sat down. Mr. Neff scratched his chin.

"Please, Mr. Neff," Cat said. "It's very important that we go back and get it right away." She glanced at Sam. Sam nodded at her.

"All right," Mr. Neff said finally. "You can go get Candy's camera. But you can't go back to the cave alone. Once was dangerous enough. We'll all go."

Andy groaned loudly. "Are you serious?" he said. "The tour is practically over and now I have to drag you guys all the way back to the beginning?"

"Sorry, Hammy," Mr. Neff said. "Muffin's camera is very important to him."

"Andy and Egg, you mean," Andy said. "Fine, let's go."

In a huff, the tour guide started back toward the mouth of the cave.

BIG TONY

"I suppose this will make sense soon," I whispered to Sam as we walked toward the front of the group.

"It sure will," Sam said. "There's just one more thing I need to know. Hold on."

Sam jogged up next to Mr. Neff. "Say, Mr. Neff," she said. "When did that new bus driver start?"

"What?" Mr. Neff said. "Oh, you mean Big Tony? Last week, I think."

"Has he done much bus driving before?" Sam asked.

"I think so," Mr. Neff said. "He used to drive for a different school, but I guess he quit when he heard about our opening."

"Thanks, Mr. Neff," Sam said. Then she joined the three of us. "That settles it."

"Settles what?" I asked.

Sam just smiled at me.

Soon we were back inside the cave. "I think the camera is over there," Sam said. She took my elbow. "Come on."

Sam pulled me right past the yellow tape. "Hey!" Andy shouted. "You can't go past the tape."

"Oh, it's just a step or two," Sam said. "There's the camera, just around the bend."

"Stop!" Mr. Neff said. "It's too dangerous."

But we hurried around the corner. There, stooped down along the cave wall, hacking away with a tiny little hammer, was Big Tony, the new bus driver.

"What are you up to?" Sam said. She put her fists on her hips and smirked at Tony.

Tony's face went pale. Quickly, he tried to cover by smiling. It looked very difficult for him. Clearly this was not a man who smiled often.

Big Tony picked up a big paper bag just by his feet. "I'm just eating my lunch," he said.

Sam and I glanced at the little hammer in his hand. He pulled it behind his back. His smile got a little smaller.

Mr. Neff and Andy came running up.

"You two are in big trouble," Mr. Neff said. His face was red with anger.

"Yup," Andy said, nodding. "We'll have to kick you out of the whole place."

Sam started to respond, but Mr. Neff cut her off and turned to Tony. "And you, Tony," he said. "I think your days as a bus driver are over."

"I can explain," Tony started.

Mr. Neff went on, "I understand if you want to eat lunch alone, but coming back here sets a bad example for the children."

Tony's face brightened. Mr. Neff actually believed he was just eating his lunch!

"Um, yes," Tony said. "You're absolutely right. I'll just grab my lunch and get out of here." He started to walk off with the bag.

"Hey!" Sam shouted.
"You dirty liar.
You can't just walk off."

Mr. Neff shot her a look. "Watch your mouth," he said. "Besides, you're in trouble too. Bigger trouble than Big Tony."

"Yeah," Tony said. As he walked past us, he stuck his tongue out at me and Sam. He was getting away with it!

WORTHLESS?

"He's got some nerve," Sam said to me. She was practically growling, like a mad dog.

But luck was on the side of justice. The bottom of Tony's paper bag began to tear.

An instant later, a colorful collection of gems and stones began to tumble from the bag. They dropped to the path and rolled toward the mouth of the cave.

"Hey!" Andy said. He ran over to Big Tony. "What is all this?"

Sam grabbed Mr. Neff's wrist. "This is what we've been trying to show you," she said. "Tony faked the cave-in so he could easily sneak in and harvest those gems."

Mr. Neff scratched his head. "But that's impossible," he said. "The rocks in this cave are totally worthless." He walked over and picked up a handful of gems. "These stones are very valuable."

"Seems like that's what everyone thought," Sam said. She turned on my camera and showed Mr. Neff the shots I'd taken. "But when Egg's flash captured these pictures," Sam went on, "it was obvious everyone was wrong about what was in the cave."

"Look at that," Mr. Neff said. "The light from your flash showed all the glittering colors in the cave walls along the closed section."

"Exactly," Sam said. By then, the rest of our class had then crossed the yellow tape and was standing around watching. Gum and Cat stood with me and Sam.

"But the cave-in," Mr. Neff said. "What does that have to do with gems?"

"Simple," Sam said. "Gum figured that out."

"Well, sort of," Gum said. He pulled a rock from his pocket. "I found this."

Andy stepped up and grabbed the rock. "Give me that," he snapped. Then he stood for a minute, staring at the rock. "This is a volcanic rock. You didn't find this here."

"That's the point," Gum said. "It shouldn't be here. There are a bunch of them, though."

"So someone faked the cave-in," Mr. Neff said.

"Big Tony did," I said.

Tony laughed. "Impossible," he said. "How could I have? They closed this section days ago. I only got here this morning with you bratty kids."

"That confused us too," Sam said. "But it had to be Tony."

Cat handed over the copy of *Gems and Jewels Price Guide Monthly*. "Tony was reading this on the bus," she said.

"We knew Big Tony was the culprit," Sam said. "We just didn't see how he managed to fake the cave-in."

"Then we remembered he started as bus driver just after you told us about this trip, last Tuesday," I said. "Tony had plenty of time to get the job and come down here to set up the fake cave-in."

"You can't prove any of that," Big Tony said.

Sam shrugged. "We don't have to prove it," she said. "We caught you red-handed stealing those gems, remember?"

"Oh, right," Tony said. "Darn it."

Andy took Big Tony by the wrist and hauled him out of the cave. The class followed. I squinted against the afternoon sun.

"What is going on here?" a rough old voice said. A figure was walking toward us — limping, actually.

"Andrew Buckaroo!" the man said. "What are you doing to that big, bearded man?"

"You're Mesquite Buckaroo," Mr. Neff said. I couldn't believe he got that name right, but had trouble with ours!

"Darn tootin' I am,"
the old man said.

He moved quicker than his teenage great-grandson. Soon he was inside the cave. He spotted the pile of gems on the ground.

"I can explain, Great-grandpa," Andy said.

He told Mr. Buckaroo all about the faked cave-in and the gems.

"Gems?" Mr. Buckaroo repeated. "You mean there are riches in these caverns after all?"

Mr. Neff nodded. "And you have these kids to thank for not letting Big Tony get away with his plan," he said.

Mr. Buckaroo looked at me and my friends.

"You four?" the old man said, leaning on his walking stick.

Then he reached down and scooped up four gems.

"A reward," he said. He dropped one gem into each of our hands. "And you're welcome back at the caverns whenever you like, no charge."

"Thank you, Mr. Buckaroo," Sam said. "But we can't accept these."

"We can't?" Gum said out of the side of his mouth.

"Nonsense," Mr. Buckaroo said. "You've earned that reward, young lady." He nodded firmly, then turned around and walked back toward the big main building.

"Mr. Neff," Cat said. She looked at the bright green gem in her palm. "I want to donate this to the bat sanctuary."

Mr. Neff's face lit up with a big smile. He took the gem and stammered, "That's very thoughtful of you, Cat."

"You got my name right!" Cat said. "I just thought it seemed fitting. After all, these gems belonged to the bats before they belonged to Mr. Buckaroo."

She glanced at me, Gum, and Sam.

Sam looked at her own gem, a bright red one, and then handed it to Mr. Neff. "Me too," she said. "For the bats."

My gem was yellow. I gave it one last look before handing it to Mr. Neff too. "Here you go," I said.

Gum sighed. He tossed his blue gem in his palm a couple of times. "Fine," he said. "Me too. But we better get extra credit for this!"

Mr. Neff laughed. "Sure," he said. "The four of you can work together on a short research paper about the local bats."

"What?" Gum said. "That sounds like more of a punishment."

"Well," Mr. Neff said. He put the gems in his pocket. "You did cross the yellow tape, after all. Seems fair to me."

Gum gritted his teeth as Mr. Neff and the rest of the class walked toward the bus. A police car had pulled up and was taking Big Tony away.

Sam put a hand on Gum's shoulder. "They say crime doesn't pay," she said.

Gum nodded. "Crime solving doesn't either," he said sadly.

• TUESDAY, APRIL 14, 20

literary news

MYSTERIOUS WRITER REVEALED!

Steve Brezenoff lives in St. Paul, Minnesota, with his wife, Beth, their son, Sam, and their small, smelly dog, Harry. Besides writing books, he enjoys playing video games, riding his bicycle, and helping middle-school students work on their writing skills. Steve's ideas almost always come to him in his dreams, so he does his best writing in his pajamas.

arts & entertainment

CALIFORNIA ARTIST IS KEY TO SOLVING MYSTERY – POLICE SAY

Marcos Calo lives happily in A Coruña, Spain, with his wife, Patricia (who is also an illustrator), and their daughter, Claudia. When Marcos and Patricia aren't drawing, they like to go on long walks by the sea. They also watch a lot of films and eat Nutella sandwiches. Yum!

A Detective's Dictionary

admission (ad-MISH-uhn)—the price to enter

collapsing (kuh-LAPS-ing)—falling down

debris (duh-BREE)—the scattered pieces of something that has been broken or destroyed

donate (DOH-nate)—give

evidence (EV-uh-duhnss)—information or facts that help prove something

gems (JEMZ)—jewels or precious stones

harvest (HAR-vist)—collecting or gathering

incriminate (in-KRIM-uh-nate)—show that someone is guilty

investigate (in-VESS-tuh-gate)—find out about something

motive (MOH-tiv)—reason for doing something

sanctuary (SANGK-choo-er-ee)—a place where animals or birds are safe from hunters

suspect (SUHS-pekt)—a person who may be responsible for a crime

temporary (TEM-puh-rer-ee)—lasting for a short time

versions (VUR-zhuhnz)—different or changed forms of something

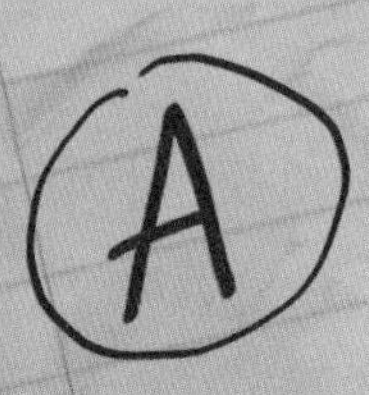

Egg Garrison
Science Class

Bats

The coolest thing about bats, in my opinion, is that they are the only mammals who are able to fly. There are other mammals, like flying squirrels, who seem to fly, but they don't, really. Not bats! Bats really can fly.

Bats have a bad reputation. People think of them as creepy creatures who live in dungeons and turn into vampires and drink blood and spread disease. But in fact, most bats eat insects! The ones who don't eat insects mostly eat fruit. It's true that vampire bats do exist, but out of more than 1,100 species of bats in the world, there are only three species of vampire bats. They live in North and South America, but not in the United States.

Just like butterflies and bees, bats spend a lot of time pollinating flowers and trees. Most people don't know that bats are very important in the ecosystem for doing things like spreading fruit seeds.

Bats can range from very small (the Kitti's Hog-Nosed Bat is about an inch long) to very big (the Giant Golden-crowned Flying Fox is thirteen inches long and weighs three pounds).

All in all, I think bats are really cool animals.

Sandwich: This is a great essay on bats. Very informative! I'm giving you ten extra-credit points. You and your friends did a wonderful thing when you donated your gems to the bat sanctuary. Maybe we can go there on a field trip sometime soon.

-Mr. Neff

FURTHER INVESTIGATIONS

CASE #FTMIOCBC

1. In this book, Mr. Neff's science class (including me) went on a field trip. What field trips have you gone on? Which one was your favorite, and why?

2. Why was a science class visiting Buckaroo Caverns? Where else might a science class go on a field trip?

3. Gum always thinks Anton is a suspect. Who else could have been a suspect in this mystery?

IN YOUR OWN DETECTIVE'S NOTEBOOK . . .

1. If Mesquite Buckaroo gave you a precious gem, what would you do with it?

2. Come up with a list of funny nicknames like the ones Mr. Neff gives everyone. What would yours be? What about your best friend?

3. This book is a mystery story. Write your own mystery story!

WAIT!
DON'T close the book!
There's MORE!
FIND MORE:
Games
Puzzles
Heroes
Villains
Authors
Illustrators at...
www.
capstonekids
.com
Still want MORE?
Find cool websites and more books like this one at www.Facthound.com.
Just type in the Book ID: 9781434232274
and you're ready to go!